Wo

Siren Green

Roderick Hunt

Illustrated by Alex Brychta

Oxford University Press

OXFORD

UNIVERSITY PRESS

Great Clarendon Street, Oxford OX2 6DP

Oxford New York
Auckland Bangkok Buenos Aires Cape Town Chennai
Dar es Salaam Delhi Hong Kong Istanbul Karachi Kolkata
Kuala Lumpur Madrid Melbourne Mexico City Mumbai
Nairobi São Paulo Shanghai Taipei Tokyo Toronto

Oxford is a registered trade mark of Oxford University Press

© text Roderick Hunt 1999
© illustrations Alex Brychta

First Published 1999

10 9 8 7 6

ISBN 0 19 918739 8

Printed in Hong Kong

Chapter 1

The cat lay by the wall in the sun. Andy stopped and looked at it. Then he bent down. 'Here cat,' he called, softly.

At once the cat stood up. It gave a miaow and walked over slowly. Andy held out his hand. The cat rubbed its head against Andy's arm.

The cat had soft brown fur. Its face was wide with large, yellow eyes. Andy noticed it had a red collar.

Andy picked the cat up. He held it in his arms and stroked its ears. 'You're beautiful,' he said. At once, the cat began to purr.

After a time, Andy put the cat down. He went up the steps up to his flat.

The door to the flat was locked.
His mum must be late. As he
unlocked the door he saw the cat. It
had followed him home.

The cat walked inside. It began to
sniff the kitchen floor. Andy looked
at it. 'Haven't you got a home?' he
asked. He poured some milk into a
saucer. 'Here cat,' he said.

He watched the cat lapping the
milk. Then he had an idea. 'If you're
lost, you can live here,' he said.

Chapter 2

Andy's mum was cross. She looked at the cat lying on the carpet.

The cat looked back at her with its yellow eyes.

'You can't just bring cats home and keep them,' said his mum. 'That's stealing.'

'I didn't bring it home,' said Andy. 'It followed me.'

'Well, it belongs to someone,' said his mum. 'Look at its collar. Its name is Siren Green.'

'That's a funny name for a cat,' said Andy.

'It belongs to Mrs Green,' said his mum. 'It lives at 3, Wolf Street. Come on. We'll take it back. We can't keep it here any longer.'

Andy didn't want to go, but his
mum made him. They carried the cat
back to its home.

Mrs Green came to the door. She
was glad to see Siren.

'She's a Burmese,' she said. 'She's a lovely cat. She's so friendly. She'll go off with anyone. I thought she was gone for good.'

Chapter 3

Andy often saw Siren Green after that. The cat was always in the same place. She liked to sit by the wall of the car park. Andy would often stop and stroke her.

'See that cat?' Andy said to Gizmo one day. 'She's called Siren.'

Siren got up and rubbed herself against Andy's legs.

'It's an odd place for a cat to sit,' said Gizmo. 'I hope she doesn't get run over by a car.'

Andy's flat was above a shop in Market Street. Gizmo lived above the shop next door. There was a car park behind the shops.

A car pulled into the car park. Gizmo pointed at the number plate. 'Hey!' he said. 'That car has got my initials - MJH - Matthew John Harding. That's smart!'

'So why does everyone call you Gizmo?' asked Andy.

'I don't know,' said Gizmo.

Andy and Gizmo began to walk towards the flats. As they did so a man and woman got out of the car.

Andy looked back. The man and woman were bending down. They were stroking Siren.

'That cat will make friends with anyone,' said Andy.

Chapter 4

Chris and Gizmo were at Andy's. They were watching TV.

Someone came to the door. It was Mrs Green. 'Have you seen Siren?' she asked.

'Not since Monday,' said Andy. 'She was in the car park. Why?'

Mrs Green looked upset. 'She's been missing for two days,' she said. 'I hope she hasn't been stolen.'

'Stolen?' said Chris. 'Who would want to steal a cat?'

'People do,' said Mrs Green. 'Cats like Siren are valuable.'

'Another cat went missing this week,' said Gizmo.

'How do you know?' asked Andy's mum.

'It was on a card in our shop window,' said Gizmo.

Gizmo's dad had a shop. The window was full of cards. People put the cards in if they wanted things, or had things to sell.

'The card said the cat was missing,' Gizmo went on.

'Well, try not to worry,' said Andy's mum. 'Cats often wander off. Maybe Siren will turn up.'

Andy thought back. 'I saw two people stroking her,' he said. 'Do you think they were cat thieves?'

'Oh dear,' said Mrs Green. 'I hope not.'

Chapter 5

Later, Andy's mum sent him to buy some milk. Gizmo went with Andy.

There was a long queue at the check-out. Everyone in the queue had a load of shopping. Andy sighed. All he had to pay for was a carton of milk.

A man at the check-out was talking. 'I wish he'd hurry up,' said Andy.

Gizmo started to tell a joke. 'Where does a frog hang its coat?' he asked.

Andy wasn't listening to Gizmo. The man at the check-out was saying something. Andy heard the word '*stolen*'. Then the man said, ' . . . *cat burglars in the area.*'

'A croak room,' said Gizmo. 'Get it? Where a frog hangs his coat.'

'Sssh!' said Andy. 'I want to hear what that man's saying.'

Gizmo looked hurt. 'My joke wasn't that bad,' he said. 'Besides! It's rude to listen to other people.'

'Sorry,' said Andy. 'But don't you see? That proves it!'

'Proves what?' asked Gizmo.

'That Mrs Green's cat has been stolen. Didn't you hear what that man said? There are cat thieves in the area.'

Chapter 6

The next day Andy, Chris and Gizmo met Loz. 'I'm going up to Gran's,' said Loz, 'Do you want to come? We can play in the den.'

The den was an old air-raid shelter in Gran's garden.

As they walked up Wolf Street they met Najma.

Andy told everyone about Siren
Green.

'There are cat thieves in the area,'
said Gizmo.

'I'll tell my auntie,' said Chris.
'She's got a Siamese cat.'

20

A car went past. It was going very slowly. The driver was looking at the houses. Gizmo looked at it. 'MJH - it's that car with my number plate again,' he said.

The car turned into Canal Street. Andy gasped. 'It's the people we saw stroking Siren,' he said. He began to run.

'Where are you going?' called Loz.

'Come on,' yelled Andy. 'They could be the cat thieves. Let's see where they're going.'

Andy ran to the corner. The car had stopped in the road near Gran's house.

Chapter 7

Andy crouched down by a wall.
'Keep down,' he called to the others.

The man got out of the car. He looked at Mr Morgan's house.

'Has Mr Morgan got a cat?' whispered Gizmo.

'Yes,' said Loz. 'He's got a cat called Blackie.'

The man bent down. Then he got back in the car.

'Did you see what he was doing?' asked Najma.

'Maybe he's taken Mr Morgan's cat,' said Chris.

'How can we find out?' asked Andy.

The woman turned the car around. She began to drive back towards Wolf Street. She slowed to a stop at the corner.

Chris had an idea. 'You look in the car,' he hissed to the others. 'Excuse me,' he called to the woman.

The woman wound the window down.

'Sorry to bother you,' said Chris. 'Could you tell us the time, please?'

The woman looked at her watch. 'It's five past ten,' she said.

The others darted across the road. They looked into the car. On the back seat was a box. It had holes in the side.

Chapter 8

The gang was in the den. They were talking about the box they had seen in the car.

'It was a cat box,' said Andy. 'It had holes to let the cat breathe.'

'I'm not sure,' said Chris. 'I think the holes were for carrying the box.'

'And we didn't really see anyone steal a cat,' said Najma.

'So what do we do now?' asked Kat.

'We know the number of the car,' said Gizmo. 'And we know what the people look like.'

Loz's Gran came into the den. She had some drinks and biscuits.

Loz told her about the man and woman. 'We think they may be cat thieves.'

Gran told them off. 'You don't know they are cat thieves,' she said. 'None of you saw them *steal* a cat.'

'But Gran,' said Loz, 'what if we are right?'

Gran was cross. 'No, Loz,' she said, firmly.

Someone came to the den. It was Mr Morgan. He called down the steps. 'Has anyone seen Blackie? I can't find her anywhere.'

Chapter 9

That night Andy slept badly. After a long time, he sat up. He looked at his watch. It was five o'clock.

Quietly, he got out of bed and crept into the living room. He found a pencil and a big pad of paper.

Then he began to draw.

Chapter 10

Andy's drawing was of a man's face. He showed it to the others.

'It's the cat thief, all right,' said Chris. 'It looks just like him.'

'How about the woman?' asked Kat. 'Did you draw her, too?'

Andy showed them another drawing. 'I did try,' he said, 'but she was much harder to draw. I couldn't get her eyes right.'

'It's not bad,' said Kat.

Najma had an idea. She asked Andy if she could borrow the drawings.

'I can scan these into our computer,' she said. 'My dad showed me how to do it.'

'But why?' asked Andy.

'Well,' said Najma. 'We know the number of the car. Now, we have pictures of the cat thieves.'

'What are you getting at?' asked Gizmo.

'Posters,' said Najma.

Chapter 11

Inspector Webb looked at the man and woman angrily. She held up a poster. It said, *'Beware of Cat Thieves.'* Underneath was Andy's drawing of the man and woman.

The man looked unhappy. The woman cleared her throat.

'Yes,' said the woman. 'We've seen them. They're all over the place.'

Inspector Webb threw the poster on her desk. 'What sort of detectives are you? I send you on an undercover job and what happens? You appear on posters all over Wolf Hill.'

'Sorry, Inspector,' said the man. 'We just don't know how it happened.'

'The poster even gives the number of your car,' said Inspector Webb. 'Well, I'm taking you off the case.'

'But, Inspector . . . ' began the woman.

'I've got another job for you. Try not to mess this one up,' went on the Inspector.

'What sort of job?' asked the man, nervously.

'Find out who put up these posters.'

Chapter 12

Detectives Watson and Sharpe went to Mr Saffrey's house. They showed Mr Saffrey one of the posters.

'Could any children in your school draw like this?' asked Detective Watson.

Mr Saffrey looked at the poster. 'We do have a boy who draws like this,' he said. 'Andy Freeman.'

'Could he have made these posters?' asked Detective Sharpe.

'Well yes,' said Mr Saffrey. 'He and his friends could have done it.'

'Well, well,' said Detective Watson.

Mr Saffrey looked at the poster again. He couldn't help smiling. 'These are drawings of you,' he said. 'They're quite good.'

Detective Sharpe sighed.

'What is this all about?' asked Mr Saffrey.

'A lot of houses have been broken into,' said Detective Watson. 'There's a cat burglar at work. He always breaks in during the day. We were hoping to catch him.'

'These posters have blown our cover,' said Detective Sharpe.

'But why would Andy think you're *cat thieves*?' asked Mr Saffrey.

'We don't know,' said Detective Sharpe. 'That's what we mean to find · out.'

Chapter 13

Andy and friends were outside Gran's house.

Suddenly a police car pulled up. Everyone looked at it. 'Oh no,' said Najma. 'It's the cat thieves!'

Detective Sharpe got out of the car. 'All right,' he called. 'We're the police. We want to talk to you.'

'Whose idea was this?' asked Detective Watson. She held up a poster.

'We all thought of it,' said Andy. 'We thought you were cat thieves.'

'Well, we're not,' said Detective Sharpe. 'We're looking for a cat burglar. That's someone who breaks into houses. He gets in and out like a cat. It's not someone who steals cats.'

'Putting up these posters was a bad idea,' said Detective Watson. 'You have no proof that any cats have been stolen.'

'You must take all the posters down,' said Detective Sharpe. 'Have you got any left?'

Najma went red. 'I've got some at home,' she said. 'Shall I go and get them?'

'Yes please,' said Detective Sharpe. 'Be as quick as you can.'

'I'll come with you,' said Kat.

It was a good job Najma and Kat went when they did.

Chapter 14

The old woman turned out of Najma's gate and hurried down Wolf Street. She carried a heavy-looking bag.

'That's funny,' said Najma. 'Did that old lady come out of our gate?'

'I didn't see,' said Kat. 'But I saw her earlier on. I'm sure that bag was empty, then.'

A sudden thought struck Najma. She ran back down Canal Street. 'Quickly!' she yelled. 'I've seen something suspicious. I think it's the cat burglar.'

Detective Sharpe ran. Detective Watson jumped into the car. She began to turn it round.

Detective Sharpe sprinted into Wolf Street. The old woman looked behind her. Then she began to run – fast!

'Stop!' shouted Detective Sharpe.

Detective Watson roared round the corner. There was a squeal of tyres. The car sped down Wolf Street. It skidded to a stop at the bottom. Detective Watson jumped out.

The old woman darted sideways into Mrs Green's garden. Siren Green was sitting on the path. She sprang up as the old woman burst through the gate. The woman tripped. There was a yell and a crash.

'Well! Well!' said Detective Sharpe. 'I think we've caught our cat burglar.'

Chapter 15

Everyone was excited. They were talking about the arrest of the cat burglar.

'I'm glad they caught him,' said Najma's dad. 'He had our video recorder in that bag. And our new answer phone.'

'You should have seen him,' laughed Najma. 'He was dressed like an old woman. Then he ran down the hill.'

'He tried to run through Mrs Green's garden,' said Andy, 'but the cat tripped him up.'

'I'm glad Siren Green hadn't been stolen,' said Gizmo. 'She had been locked in a shed.'

'There were no cat thieves, after all,' said Kat.

'No, just a cat burglar,' laughed Andy. 'In a wig!'